Buenos modales / Manners Matter

Buenos modales en el parque
Good Manners at the Playground

Melissa Raé Shofner

traducido por / translated by Eida de la Vega

ilustrado por / illustrated by
Lorna William

PowerKiDS
press.

New York

Published in 2018 by The Rosen Publishing Group, Inc.
29 East 21st Street, New York, NY 10010

First Edition

Translator: Eida de la Vega
Editorial Director, Spanish: Nathalie Beullens-Maoui
Editor, English: Melissa Raé Shofner
Book Design: Raúl Rodriguez
Illustrator: Lorna William

Cataloging-in-Publication Data

Names: Shofner, Melissa Raé.
Title: Good manners at the playground = Buenos modales en el parque / Melissa Raé Shofner.
Description: New York : PowerKids Press, 2018. | Series: Manners matter = Buenos modales | In English and Spanish | Includes index.
Identifiers: ISBN 9781508157090 (library bound)
Subjects: LCSH: Etiquette for children and teenagers–Juvenile fiction. | Playgrounds–Juvenile fiction.
Classification: LCC PZ7.S56 Goo 2018 | DDC [E]–dc23

Manufactured in the United States of America

CPSIA Compliance Information: Batch #BS17PK: For further information contact Rosen Publishing, New York, New York at 1-800-237-9932

Contenido

Contents

Amy quiere jugar fuera. "¿Podemos ir al parque, por favor?", pregunta.

Amy wants to play outside. "May we please go to the playground?" she asks.

Amy y su mamá montan sus bicicletas.

Mom and Amy ride their bicycles.

Esperan en la señal de stop.

Los conductores las dejan cruzar.

They wait at the stop sign. The drivers let them cross.

Los amigos de Amy están en el parque.

Amy's friends are at the playground.

"¡Hola!" dice Amy. "¡Vamos a jugar!".

"Hi!" she says. "Let's go play!"

Corren al tobogán.

They race to the slide.

Amy deja que Mike y Sasha vayan primero.

Amy espera su turno.

Amy let's Mike and Sasha go first.

Amy waits for her turn.

Sasha quiere montar la bicicleta de Amy.

Sasha dice, "Por favor".

Sasha wants to ride Amy's bicycle.

Sasha says, "Please."

Amy deja que Sasha use su casco.

Amy lets Sasha use her helmet.

13

Mike empuja a Amy en los columpios.

¡Sube muy alto!

Mike pushes Amy on the swings.

She goes really high!

Ahora es el turno de Mike.

Amy se ofrece a empujarlo.

Now it's Mike's turn. Amy offers to push him.

Amy ve a un niño solito.

"Ven a jugar con nosotros", le dice.

Amy sees a lonely little boy.

"Come play with us," she says.

Todos se trepan en las barras.

Everyone climbs on the monkey bars.

La mamá de Amy trajo jugo y galletas.

Amy comparte la merienda con sus amigos.

Amy's mom brought juice and cookies.

Amy shares the snacks with her friends.

Es hora de volver a casa. Amy recoge la basura.

It's time to go home. Amy cleans up the trash.

Le ayuda a Sasha a doblar la manta.

She helps Sasha fold the blanket.

"¡Gracias por jugar conmigo!", dice Amy.

"¡Hasta pronto!".

"Thank you for playing with me!" says Amy.

"See you soon!"

Palabras que debes aprender
Words to Know

(la) bicicleta
bicycle

(el) casco
helmet

(el) jugo
juice

Índice / Index

24